Left Shoe
Right Shoe

Written by
Yolanda Lopez-Rettew

Illustrated by
Bonnie Lemaire

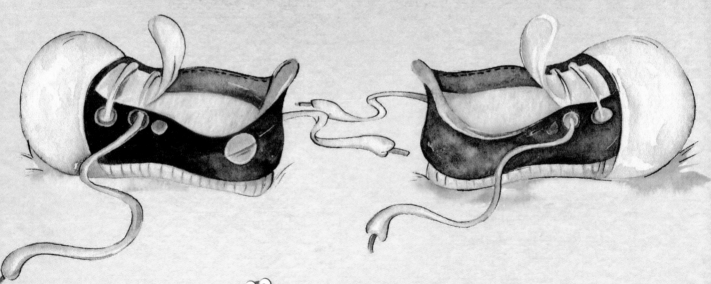

Storytime favorites

Thank you to my husband, Patrick,
for all your love and support

_____

Copyright © Text Storytime Favorites 2009
Copyright © Illustrations Bonnie Lemaire 2009

All rights reserved. No part of this book may be reproduced in any
manner without the written consent of the publisher except for
brief excerpts in critical reviews or articles.

ISBN: 978-0-9821160-0-5
Library of Congress Control Number: 2009902538
10 9 8 7 6 5 4 3 2 1

Printed and bound in the USA

Book Design & Layout by Sun Editing & Book Design
www.suneditwrite.com

Published by Storytime Favorites
For information, visit www.storytimefavorites.com

For Aaron,
the magic and wonder in my life

One morning, a little boy named
Lorenzo walked into his garden. The sun
was shining and the sky was blue.
It was a beautiful day.

Lorenzo took his shoes off so he could walk on the soft green grass.

First he took off his left shoe.

Then he took off his right shoe.

A ladybug landed on a flower in the garden.

She was bright yellow and very small.

Lorenzo had never seen a yellow ladybug before.

Lorenzo reached out to touch the little ladybug.

She flew away and landed near his left shoe.

A moment later, a rabbit hopped out of the bushes.

He sat next to Lorenzo's right shoe.

This was a special rabbit. He was red and had big floppy ears.

Lorenzo had never seen a red rabbit before.

He reached down to pet him.

Lorenzo smiled at his two new friends, the little ladybug near his left shoe and the red rabbit beside his right shoe.

Lorenzo liked his new friends, but then he felt sad. It was lunchtime, and he did not want to say goodbye.

"It would be nice if my friends could always be with me," he said.

The little ladybug was small enough to carry, but Lorenzo knew the red rabbit was too big.

What could Lorenzo do?

When the red rabbit saw Lorenzo's sad face, he had an idea.

He said, "I will make myself small like the little ladybug."

The red rabbit made a wish.

Poof!

Suddenly, the red rabbit was small like the little ladybug! His wish had come true.

Lorenzo was so pleased.

The red rabbit was pleased, too.

There was one more thing to do. The little ladybug and the red rabbit needed a safe way to travel together.

Lorenzo had a plan.

He would carry them on his shoes!

Lorenzo invited his friends to come for a ride with him. And they did.

The little ladybug flew onto his left shoe.

The red rabbit hopped onto his right shoe.

Now Lorenzo and his friends would go everywhere together.

This made them all happy.

Lorenzo heard his mom call out, "Lorenzo, come into the house for lunch.

"And remember to bring your shoes!"

The End

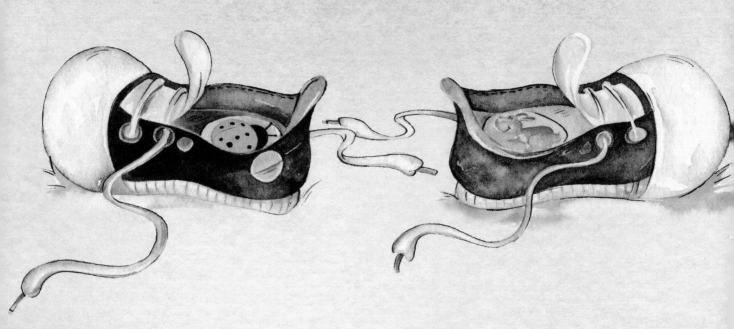